Ours to Love

The Brotherhood Series: Book 3

Nia JoLove

© **Copyright 2022 - All rights reserved.**

The content contained within this book may not be reproduced, duplicated, or transmitted without direct written permission from the author.

Legal Notice:

This book is copyright protected. It is only for personal use. You cannot amend, distribute, sell, use, quote, or paraphrase any part, or the content within this book, without the consent of the author.

Disclaimer Notice:

This is a work of fiction. Names, characters, businesses, places, events, locales, and incidents are either the products of the author's imagination or used in a fictitious manner. Any resemblance to actual persons, living or dead, or actual events is purely coincidental.

Table of Contents

Chapter 1: On Set

Chapter 2: The Men

Chapter 3: At Home

Chapter 4: We Meet

Chapter 5: On the Road

Chapter 6: Key West

Chapter 7: Cash and Zack

Chapter 8: Blaze

Chapter 9: United Front

Chapter 10: At the Restaurant

Chapter 11: Boardwalk

Chapter 12: Full Moon

Chapter 13: Crazy in Love

Chapter 14: This Isn't Working

Epilogue

Chapter 1: On Set

"Action!"

Denise moved effortlessly across the room. She pulled her co-star close and dragged her full lips across his mouth. His woodsy scent mingled in her nostrils. She let him grab her ass and back her against the wall. He stood a foot taller than her. His dreads fell to his shoulders. His dark mocha skin glistened in the light. He pressed his massive thigh between her legs, slightly brushing her sensitive mound. Denise let out a little moan. She let him take the lead with the kiss.

"Cut! Cut! Cut!" shouted the director.

"Damn, just when it was about to get good," said her co-star with a bulging erection visible through his black slacks.

Denise licked her lips and straightened her fiery red gown.

"That's a wrap for today. Good job, everyone," said the smiling director. "Tomorrow we prep for the sex scene. Denise and Eric, keep that chemistry going. We're going to need that and more to keep the audience captivated."

Eric leaned closer to Denise and whispered in her ear, "Hey, let's finish this in my trailer," as he rubbed a finger down her arm.

"Hell, no," said Denise as she pushed past him. "You know I don't like you like that. Plus, ain't nobody on this set touching my pussy unless they've won an Oscar."

Then she strutted away to her trailer leaving Eric looking shocked and appalled.

Denise entered her trailer, locked the door, and slid down on the couch. Her dress rode up, exposing long caramel legs. She knew she could have been nicer to Eric, but she had to keep up the appearance that she was a diva. She had built her acting career on that fact. Ever since her parents passed away in a tragic accident when she was five years old, she had to pretend. She pretended to be happy, when she wasn't. She pretended to be okay when mentally she wasn't. She pretended to be strong but often times felt weak.

    Now, that's what she did for a living. She pretended for a worldwide audience. But no one knew the kind, caring, and lovable Denise. Only her sister Jasmine. She didn't have to pretend with her. She could be her true self. Jasmine was always there protecting and defending Denise from whomever and whatever. Denise thought about her parents a lot. What would they think of her? Would they be proud of the path she had chosen? She enjoyed acting. It was something she had wanted to do since she was a child. After her parents died, she'd consumed TV like it was life. Her grandma took care of Denise and Jasmine but was strict, stern, and not very lovable. TV was an outlet for Denise. She would watch shows like *My Wife and Kids* and *Everybody Hates Chris*. Movies captivated her even more. She could remember line after line of *Coming to America* and would recite it to Jasmine.

Denise ran her hand through her loose curly hair. Life was going well, but she was missing something. She couldn't put her finger on what it was.

Her phone rang. Denise grabbed it off the nearby table. She didn't recognize the number but answered it anyway.

"Hello? Hello?" She could hear heavy breathing on the other end.

"Who is this? Hello!"

More heavy breathing ensued. Then the caller hung up. That was the second call like that this week. Denise's heart started to race. She closed her eyes. What the hell is going on? thought Denise. Two calls and heavy breathing. The phone began to ring again. Denise hesitated to pick it up. Noticing that it was Jasmine, she pushed the green button.

"Hey, Sis, how are things going?"

Jasmine sounded very happy and, of course, she would be. She had married the men of her dreams and had a family who loved and cherished her.

"Things are going okay."

"Denise, what's wrong? You sound distracted."

"I...I.... just received another call, and the person didn't say anything but was breathing heavily."

"What the hell! Another call? What is going on?"

8

"I don't know," said Denise while shaking her head even though her sister couldn't see it.

"It started about two weeks ago. The first call was like this one with heavy breathing. I didn't think much about it until it happened today right before you called."

"You know, if I find out who this bastard is, it will be over. I can't have anyone bothering my sister."

"Thanks, Jasmine, for having my back. You've always been there for me even when we were kids."

"You know it! Denise, maybe it's something or maybe it's nothing, but you need to call the police."

Denise looked at the plush carpet in her trailer.

"What if I call the police and it's nothing or just some kids playing games?"

"You're right. How about telling your manager? Maybe he can get someone like a bodyguard to protect you."

"That sounds like a plan. Having an extra person to watch my back would be great. Okay, enough worrying about me, how are you doing? You sounded so happy when you answered the phone."

"Yes, Denise, I am happy. The men treat me like a queen. They take care of me physically and sexually, and it is amazing!"

"Can I ask you something?"

"Yes, anything."

"How does the sex physically work?"

Jasmine paused, "Denise, we have three openings, and my men make sure to fill them all."

Both ladies burst into laughter.

"But on a serious note, Denise, it's more than the sex with them. It's a connection like no other. We don't keep anything from each other. As unconventional as it may be, we are a family unit in all the ways that matter."

"So, when are the babies coming?"

"Whoa, pump the brakes. I need time to enjoy the marriage and the men. It's all still so new. But my men are ready to fill the house with little ones."

"Jasmine, I am so happy for you, and you know Mom and Dad would be proud as well."

"I'm proud of you, Denise. You went after your dream, and now you are a star. Our parents would have been proud."

The phone went silent for a moment as the women thought about their parents.

"Denise, take care. If you need anything, call, and I will be there."

Denise smiled, "I know you will."

"Bye, Jasmine."

"Bye, Denise."

I gotta get out of here, thought Denise. It was getting late, and she had to be back early in the morning. Denise locked her trailer and jumped in her car which was parked nearby.

Chapter 2: The Men

Blaze angled the gun and gently squeezed the trigger. It kicked back against his shoulder as it released the bullet. The bullet hit the paper target with a pop. His legs were planted firmly, so he didn't move as he fired another round.

The AK- 47 assault rifle was powerful, but Blaze was six feet four and 276 pounds of pure power himself.

This was his scene.

He wiped the moisture from his hand on his black-clad jeans and returned his hand to the trigger.

He focused and squeezed the trigger.

The more he squeezed, the better he felt. He had a lot going on in his head and knew that a day at the firing range with his brothers would help.

His thoughts drifted to his days in the marines. He was 19 and dumb when he joined. He had gotten into a lot of trouble and needed to escape, so he jumped in when the recruiter at his school suggested it.

Plus, it was the perfect way to carry a gun and not get looked at like he was a thug.

Guns were his thing. He knew everything about them. How to shoot'em, how to clean them, and what made them work. That was his advantage in the marines. He was the best shot out of everyone in his class, so they made him a sniper. He stayed in the marines and gained rank.

After a while, he was sent to Afghanistan where he fought side by side with Cash and Zack. They became fast friends on and off the battlefield. They watched each other's backs and helped each other during hard times.

Cassius also known as Chase was the pretty boy with the money.

You could tell he had money by the way he carried himself. He had joined the military to escape his family business. His family still supported him to a degree but had turned their backs on him after he'd said that he wanted another life and career choice.

Zack, on the other hand, came from the streets. He was a fighter from the day he was born. He fought in underground boxing matches in New York. That all changed when 9/11 happened. He'd stopped fighting people on the streets and joined the Marine Corps to fight for his country.

After being in Afghanistan, it changed them all. They drank a lot, had sex a lot, and were broken.

Separately, they couldn't shake the demons from the past. But together they had a fighting chance. They bonded over their pain and suffering. No one understood what they had been through but each other. After therapy and time, they began to heal. They started a private security firm with some success. Now they were a strong family unit. But there was an important piece missing—a woman to love.

They tried having separate women, but they were always away guarding someone out of state and country. It was hard for them to have a long-distance relationship. In time, the women would feel neglected and would ultimately cheat or simply leave.

After the marines, they shared everything. A home, their fears, and, eventually, their women. But most women couldn't and didn't want to be shared by three horny-as-hell men and be in such an unconventional relationship. But the men held out hope that one day, they would find someone they could share and love. They believed that this was the way to stay together as a family and provide support for each other.

"Blaze, get out of your head, man, and shoot the damn shot," said Zack, pulling Blaze from the past to focus on the target. "I told you this fool was daydreaming."

"Don't worry about me," Blaze said. "You know I got this." He replaced his ear protection and finished shooting the target until the paper looked like confetti.

"Now that's what I'm talking about," said Cash as he playfully punched Blaze in the back.

"Let's get the hell out of here," said, Zack. "I'm tired of watching Blaze show off. Plus, we have some work to do."

The men jumped into the dark blue BMW SUV and headed back to their office.

At the office, they discussed a new case.

"We got a call today from an actress's manager."

"Oh, no," said Blaze, "not another celebrity client. These celebrities are too snobby and never listen or do what is required to protect them from danger. Plus, they look at us bodyguards as the lowest common denominator on earth. Let's pass on that one."

"You know we need this case and all the others too," said Zack. He was the more level-headed one out of the three, ensuring that the team stayed focused. "We've accumulated some debt and need to pay it off soon."

"But I thought we were doing good money-wise," Cash said. He had helped finance the venture. They all put in money from their government pension.

"Yes, we are doing good, but I want it to stay like that," said Zack.

"Well, let's hear about this snobby celebrity," laughed Blaze.

"She's the actress named Denise," said Zack.

"Oh, hell nah," said Blaze. "She is the worst one. I've seen her in the news, and she is a diva."

"Yes, she is a bit of a diva, but let's see what her case is about."

Zack read that she had a possible stalker but no evidence to support it.

"Guys, it may be just a babysitting job to calm her fears. There don't seem to be any attempts on her life. Just some heavy breathing on the phone. What do you think? Plus, the money is good, and she is hot."

The guys looked at the picture in the file.

"I think we should give it a try," said Cash.

"Okay," agreed Blaze. "But the first time she gets out of hand, I'm gone."

"I'll call her manager to confirm that we will consider doing the job. He mentioned that we would be able to meet her on set tomorrow around 1:00 p.m.," said, Zack.

"Sounds like a plan," agreed Blaze and Cash.

Chapter 3: At Home

Denise looked up at the 60-story luxury high rise that she had been living in for the last month while filming *Bad Boys 5* in Miami. It was simply breathtaking the way the sun hovered over the top of the building before dipping down between the clouds. The building was impressive with multiple layers of penthouse floors, a concierge, and a gym on the first floor that focused on holistic health.

Denise put on her glasses and walked through the oversize glass doors. Of course, she was a star and needed to act like it.

"Hello, Denise," said the concierge. "Your mail has been picked up and delivered to your suite. There was a large package that we left outside your door."

Denise waved him off with a brush of her hand. This didn't bother Charles, the concierge. He was used to snooty celebrities.

Denise entered the elevator and noticed two people kissing. She tried not to stare but found herself wrapped up in the kiss.

"Do you want some too?" asked the man with dark hair and piercing brown eyes when he noticed Denise looking.

"No," said Denise.

The man continued kissing the young blond and playing in her hair. The couple reached their floor and exited the elevator.

Denise missed being in a relationship and feeling cherished. She hadn't dated in months due to her acting career and the perception that she was a diva. Her last relationship was with David. He was in the film business too. In the beginning, things were great. He wooed her with his charm and amazing looks. She didn't want to date anyone in the film industry but his relentless pursuit led her to cave in and date him. As the relationship continued, their jobs kept them apart. Eventually, David cheated on her which caused them to break up. It wasn't like a normal breakup with private tears and a bucket of ice cream. It was splattered across several publications and news outlets. Denise felt humiliated and destroyed. From that point on, she guarded her heart.

"Hey, lady," said the neighbor, pulling Denise's focus back to the present.

"Hi, Joelle," said Denise as she tried to walk past her penthouse.

Joelle was the type of neighbor who knew everyone's business, but you didn't know hers. She was in her mid-40s but looked older.

"Did you just finish filming one of those porn movies?" said Joelle as she laughed.

"Don't you mean award-nominated movie?" spat Denise.

"Whatever," said Joelle as she headed into her penthouse.

Joelle was interesting. She must have had loads of money to be living in the penthouse. But she looked like she never worked a day in her life. She was pretty secretive but nosy.

As she walked toward her apartment, Denise noticed the box lying on the floor near her door. It wasn't a big box, but it wouldn't fit in the mail slot. Grabbing the box, Denise went into her penthouse apartment. Floor-to-ceiling windows beckoned her to view the city below. It was what drew her to this penthouse. She felt like a bird perched high up. Large tile lined the floors. The furniture was modern and sleek. The kitchen was expansive even though she rarely cooked in it. She was at the top of her career. But why did she feel so lonely?

She sat on the couch to go through the mail. She wondered who could have sent her the box. Maybe Jasmine, she thought. She went to the kitchen to find the box opener. Setting the box on the counter, she noticed that it didn't have any postage. She knew that it must have been hand-delivered to the front desk. She opened the box and immediately started to scream. Her breathing stopped as she looked inside at the teddy bear covered in blood.

Denise backed away from it and found her phone to call the police. After hanging up with the police, she paced the floor waiting for their arrival.

When the doorbell rang, Denise looked through the peephole and then let the police in. The police entered the apartment, looked around, and inspected the package.

"Ma'am, are you okay?

Yes, said Denise.

We can't file a report because there doesn't seem to be any foul play. Someone may have pranked you with the teddy bear with red paint."

"I think I have a stalker," said Denise.

"What makes you think you have a stalker? This is just one isolated incident. Unless there are more incidents. Are there more?" asked the tall, slim police officer.

"Someone has been calling and breathing heavily on the phone."

"Did they say anything threatening or otherwise?"

"No, just heavy breathing."

Denise looked down at her hands.

"Well, we can't press charges because there were no threats. Did you check the phone number that was called?"

"No, it was an unknown number."

"Ma'am at this point we don't have a crime. If anything else happens, give us a call."

Then the officer and his partner left. Denise locked the door and stood against it for a moment thinking.

What should I do? The police don't think it is anything, but my gut is telling me otherwise. I need to get in touch with my manager to see what he can do.

Leaving the front door, Denise walked to the living room to get her phone that was inside her purse.

The phone rang twice before Dan picked it up.

"Hey, Denise, is everything all right?"

"Not really. I've been getting some weird calls again, and today, someone hand-delivered a teddy bear dripping in red paint to the front desk for me."

"Denise, did you call the police?"

"Yes, but they couldn't file a report because a crime has not been committed."

"Denise, don't worry. I have already called a private security firm that can watch your back. It could be some weirdo who's trying to scare you."

"Yes, you're probably right."

"I'll tell the firm to meet you on set tomorrow."

"Thanks, Dan."

"No problem, Denise."

Then they both hung up.

Looking around, she took a deep breath and exhaled. Denise felt like she could breathe a little easier knowing that someone would be watching over her. She was still uneasy about what had taken place but eventually fell asleep in her bed.

Chapter 4: We Meet

Denise moved her hips in a circular motion as she straddled her co-star. She pumped her ass up and down as if she was riding a horse. She could feel his rock-hard cock press against her core through the almost invisible flesh-colored thong that she wore. He moaned and grabbed her hair to pull her in for a long hard kiss. He caressed her breast first slowly then roughly.

"Cut, cut, cut," said the director. "We got the footage that we needed. That's a wrap for today. We will finish shooting the ending in one week. Enjoy the time off. You all deserve it."

The co-star released her lips. But he thrust his hips so he could feel Denise's pussy before she got up. He smiled as the revelation of what he was doing became apparent on

Denise's face. She didn't smile back but frowned.

"I told you to stop messing around, Eric."

"But you know I like you, and he like you too," Eric said, pointing to his dick.

"Let me get the hell off your crazy ass."

Denise fastened her robe to cover the lacy black lingerie top and skin-tone thong underneath. She left the bed and headed to her trailer, but while she was crossing the set, she saw three men walking her way.

Her breath caught as they approached. She didn't know why she was reacting this way to not one, but three men. Maybe it was the physical attraction. The deep-chocolate giant of a man was built like a cannon ready to shoot off. His bald head glistened under the stage lights, and his bearded face reward her with a large smile. The other two men were hot as hell too. Both men were about the same size but one had a slightly bulkier build with wide shoulders. One of the men had skin the color of mocha chocolate while the other had caramel skin. The man with the caramel skin looked like he was of Spanish and African heritage, and it could be seen in his strong jawline. The mocha skinned man had short hair and a full beard. His lips looked like they could do some damage on her body.

The men stood in front of Denise. They towered over her as she was only 5'8" with heels. The tallest man spoke with a baritone voice.

"Hello, Denise, my name is Blaze."

He reached for her hand to shake it. As their hands touched, a spark was elicited. Blaze had never felt anything like it before. Yes, Denise was beautiful, but there was something else about her that he couldn't put his finger on. With hesitation, he let go of her hand.

"Your manager told us you were having some trouble, and he said that you may need protection. Do you have a private place where we can talk?"

"Yes, but I don't know about all this," said Denise. "Does there need to be three of you?"

"Yes, my brothers will be needed to help protect you around the clock. We take shifts."

"Okay," said Denise with reservation. "You know I haven't hired any of you yet, so we will have to see."

Denise escorted the men to her trailer at the back of the set.

Blaze, Zack, and Cash noticed how her hips swayed as she walked. Underneath the thin silk robe, caramel creamy long legs peeked out. Denise was beautiful, and the men knew it. Cash looked at Blaze to see if he saw the same. Blaze shook his head in acknowledgment.

The men and Denise filed into the trailer. Once inside, Denise realized how small it was. The men made it feel crowded. They sat arm to arm on the couch while she sat in the chair.

"Hello, Denise. My name is Zack. This is Cash, and you just met Blaze. We are former marines and now the owners of a private security firm."

Zack looked at Denise's eyes while they talked. He was drawn to her as well.

"We have guarded and protected politicians, celebrities, and more. Our military background provided us with the key skills to guard you. We have read your file, but tell us what's going on so we can get a better handle on the situation."

"I don't think it's that serious," said Denise as she looked at the men in front of her and nibbled her bottom lip. "There has been some heavy breathing on the phone with no words spoken. Then a package was hand-delivered with a teddy bear covered in red paint."

The men looked at each other with concerned expressions.

"Is this something you've seen before?" asked Denise.

"Yes," said Zack. "It looks like you have a stalker on your hands. First, the incidents are small but gradually get more threatening as the stalking continues."

"Whoever it may be, is trying to get your attention," said Blaze.

"Do you know anyone who wants to hurt you?" asked Cash.

"Who doesn't want to harm me?" said Denise jokingly. "As you may know, I have a bit of an attitude, and most people can't take it. I am direct, and I know what I want.

Cash looked at the beautiful woman sitting in front of him. Her hair was full of curls that framed her face. She had lingerie underneath her robe. He tried not to react to the delicate lacy fabric that teased from underneath the silk robe, but most red-blooded men wouldn't be able to resist. Just thinking about it had his groin begging to be free. He imagined her long legs wrapped around him as he pumped into her. Cash broke from the thought and continued listening to Denise.

"I was recently in a relationship, but it didn't work out. Maybe it's one of my exes doing all of this."

"Are you in a relationship now?" asked Blaze, asking the question that each man wanted to know.

"You're getting personal," said Denise.

"It's to ensure we have all the facts," said Zack.

"Well, in that case, no, I am not in a relationship. It's kind of hard when I'm flying from set to set making movies."

Cash breathed in. He didn't know why he was holding his breath while Denise answered the question about being in a relationship. He didn't know why he was happy that no one had staked their claim on her. He would have to find out what this connection was about.

"Your manager has hired us, and we will accept the job. We can start full protection tomorrow."

"Thanks," said Denise. "But don't get in my way. I am an actress first, and all this stuff is secondary."

Denise felt comfortable with the men. She didn't know that it would happen so fast.

Crash!! The sound of glass breaking startled Denise, and she screamed.

Zack quickly jumped in front and covered her with his body.

"What the hell! Son of a bitch!"

"Let's get him," said Blaze as he and Cash ran out of the trailer to catch whoever it was on foot.

Zack's body pressed against Denise didn't feel awkward. He wanted to stay covering her but got up quickly when he felt her moving.

"Are you okay, Denise?" asked Zack.

"I'm fine. That bastard is just trying to scare me."

Moments later, Blaze and Cash returned to the trailer.

"Did you see anyone?" asked Zack

"No, the person ran away too fast for us to catch up and get a clear ID on them."

"Did you see what it was that broke the window?" asked Cash.

"No," said Zack. "I wanted to make sure that Denise was safe. But let's look around now."

The guys searched the trailer for whatever broke the glass.

Alarm set in when they noticed a dead bird with its head cut off and a note tied around its body. The note read "Die Denise!"

"What the hell?!" yelled Cash.

"This is some sick shit," said Blaze.

Zack tried to shield Denise from the scene of the bird and the note, but she wanted to see. As soon as she approached the area and saw the bird, the blood drained from her face, and she went cold. She covered her mouth. The realization that someone was trying to kill her hit hard. Her body shook with anger as she paced the floor.

"Shit, shit! I can't believe this is happening. What the hell am I going to do? I can't stay here or at my place. Whoever it is, know where I live."

"We can protect you, Denise," said Zack in a calm voice. "You can stay with us until we find out who it is that is after you."

Zack rubbed her back.

"We have a vacation home in Key West. No one would know you are there. It's away from your work and home but close enough if you need to get back fast."

"We can protect you around the clock," said Blaze. "Plus, the home has a state-of-the-art security system."

"I don't know who you are," said Denise. "I can't just leave with all of you." She looked at the men as they gathered around her.

"You can trust us," said Blaze as he reached for her hand but withdrew.

"How the hell can I trust you when I just met you?"

Blaze walked up to Denise. "Who else do you have that you can stay with?" asked

Blaze. He wanted to ensure she was safe with or without them.

Denise thought about the situation. She knew that she could stay with Jasmine but didn't want to bring trouble to her door. She had already been through a lot.

"I don't have a lot of people that I trust," said Denise as she smoothed down her hair. "It seems like the only option is to go with you guys. Because right now it wouldn't work to stay here.

"Good," said Cash. "Grab some clothes and let's get the hell out of here."

Denise quickly changed, packed a bag, and left with the men. She called to tell Jasmine where she would be because she was the only one she could trust at this point besides the men.

They got into the SUV and left for Key West, Florida, which was about a three-hour drive from their current location in Miami.

Chapter 5: On the Road

Only a few cars passed by while driving along US 1. Melancholy music played in the SUV as silence ensnared each passenger. Outside the car, sparkling blue water caressed white sandy beaches while palm trees waved goodbye.

    Denise fidgeted with the passenger's side door while Zack strummed his finger on the steering wheel. He paced the car at 70 and breezed along the highway. Blaze and Cash took up much of the room in the back seat, each distracted by the phones in their hands.

    She thought about all that had happened. Was someone trying to kill her? But why? She wasn't the nicest, but she wasn't all-out cruel.

    She was still pretty rattled by the dead bird and note. She tried not to think about it too much, but the scene was on repeat in her head. Now she was going to Key West with a security team of men that she didn't know. At the time, it had felt like a good idea, but now she was having second thoughts. Her sister Jasmine knew where she was and would check on her. That would have to do for the moment. But she couldn't continue to hide from a possible stalker.

"Breaking the silence, are you sure you guys aren't trying to kidnap me to do all kinds of nasty things to?" quipped Denise. "Hell, I have seen the way you all have been looking at me." She rolled her eyes as she looked around the SUV.

Zack smiled, "We can appreciate a beautiful lady, that's all, and, Denise, you are beautiful."

He had been staring at her in the mirror while he was driving. She was indeed beautiful but it was a natural beauty. She had full lips, almond-shaped eyes, and brown skin that begged to be touched. Loose curls cascaded down her shoulders, making her look dreamy. He tried not to stare but constantly lost focus on driving because of the distraction in the passenger seat.

"Denise, relax," said Blaze as he rubbed her shoulders from the back seat. "We will take care of you, and we are gentlemen."

Blaze's caressed Denise's shoulders like she was a flower in his hands. He could be considered the gentle giant.

Denise relaxed under his ministrations. It was nice to be cared for even if it was something as simple as a shoulder rub.

She didn't want to think about the events that had happened that day, so she asked the men about themselves.

"How did you all meet?"

"We met while fighting in Afghanistan," said Cash.

Denise was shocked. She knew they were in the military but didn't realize that they had also fought in the war in Afghanistan.

"When we came back from fighting, everything was different. We had changed, and the world we knew had changed. People didn't quite understand what we went through in the war. But my brothers here did. We bonded through war and afterward. We are una familia. We came back, got healed, and now we are looking for a woman to complete the family unit."

Denise turned her head to look at Cash.

"Do you share women too?"

"'Too?'" asked Cash.

"Yes, my sister is in a relationship with three men. She married them, and now they live together in Georgia. It's unconventional, but it works."

Each man looked at Denise with a look of surprise and trepidation since they didn't know her thoughts about this type of relationship.

"We tried relationships with separate women, but it never worked because we would leave, and they would be tired of waiting. We want a relationship where, if one or two of us leave for work or any other reason, there will always be someone there to take care of our woman," Cash said.

Denise was intrigued but was unsure about the whole idea and changed the subject to lighter topics. The start of the day had been intense, but as they drove and got to know Denise, the mood lightened.

The men bantered with Denise and each other. But she didn't back down and gave as good as she took. They talked and laughed about movies, music, and any other thing that would pass the time while they drove.

"Do you remember that time when we were stationed at Camp Pendleton in

California? It was late and the restaurants on base were closed, but we were hungry," said Blaze.

"Yes, I remember," said Zack. "We had a few MREs and beers."

"What are MREs?" asked Denise.

"They're dehydrated meals in a bag. Mostly to eat during war or when food is hard to get."

"Oh hell," said Cash. "In the morning, our damn stomachs hurt so bad that we had to call the clinic and was on quarters for two days," laughed Blaze.

"What had happened?" said Denise.

"The damn MRE was about 15 years old," said Blaze. "We were so hungry we didn't check the date."

Blaze, Zack, Cash, and Denise laughed at the story.

The guys made sure Denise was smiling by keeping the conversation flowing, but the attraction was there as well, simmering underneath all the conversation.

Chapter 6: Key West

The car stopped in front of an impressive yellow and white two-story beach house on about an acre of land that backed up to the oceanfront. It was surrounded by palm trees and offered plenty of privacy. Beach homes lined the ocean, and a boardwalk was nearby that opened to restaurants and stores.

"Denise, welcome to our *casa* of Key West," said Cash.

Zack came around and helped Denise from the car.

Denise looked at the house. It was beautiful.

"This is nice," Denise said, very surprised.

She was a bit happy that she had chosen to go with the guys. She still couldn't shake the events that had happened earlier, but she tried not to let them impact her too much. Maybe this would be what she needed. She had been working hard and not having any fun. Plus, the three men were gorgeous, and each of them looked at her with raw desire. She would have to see what happened, but her priority would be to find out who her stalker could be.

"Denise, we bought this house after leaving the military as a place to escape. We normally come down here on the weekend or whenever there's a holiday," said Zack.

"It has the best security system," said Cash, "and with our protection, you will be safe."

Denise stepped into the house. The living room had vaulted ceilings with white beams that drew the eyes up. Massive dark leaf ceiling fans waving in a circular motion gave off a calm feeling. Glass doors led outside to the infinity pool that overlooked the ocean. Denise was impressed not with the house so much but with the three guys that had worked to get the house. It was an open-concept house so the kitchen, living room, and dining room were visible by looking around, and an oversized guest room was located to the left of the kitchen. Floating wood stairs with white railings led up to more bedrooms.

"Cash, show Denise to her room. Denise, after you're comfortable, we can talk strategy."

"Guys let's call contacts and see what's going on," said Zack.

Cash secured the front door and led Denise upstairs.

"This is your room," Cash said, stopping in front of a room that was in the middle of three other rooms.

They went in.

"Everything you need is here. There are extra clothes in the closet if you left something. Also, there are toiletries in the bathroom. Denise, we want you to feel comfortable while you're here."

Denise saw the sincere look in Cash's eyes.

"I know you are probably used to better accommodations, but I hope you can make this work until we help clear everything up."

Cash's sincerity affected her. She could have responded but shook her head in agreement. Normally she would say something rude but didn't have the heart.

"Thank you. I will be down soon."

Cash left the room. He stayed at the door thinking about Denise. He wanted her but didn't know why. Yes, she was a bit of a diva, but today, he didn't see it. She was strong when adversity came, and she didn't back down from a fight. The only reason she was with them was that she realized that someone was truly trying to hurt her.

Cash walked down to the living room where his fellow brothers were waiting.

"She looked pretty shaken up," said Blaze as he took a seat at the table.

"Yes, this must've rattled her," said Zack, "but we will keep her safe."

"She was quiet when I left the room, but she's strong and will get through this," said Cash.

Cash joined the other two men at the dining room table.

"You know, there is something about Denise that I just can't shake," said Cash. "There is a connection that I don't understand. I value her independence and her fight."

"Yes, I like her too," said Zack. "She's been through so much and, like us, she continues to be strong. I don't remember ever feeling like this for someone so soon."

"Maybe it's sexual," said Blaze in a questioning voice, "but there is something else that I feel."

"What should we do?" asked Blaze.

"Maybe we should get to know her. Let her see what sharing her would look like by protecting her and being there for her."

"Yes, but should we fuck her too?" asked Blaze jokingly.

The room went from a serious tone to a more normal brother banter.

"Seems like that's what you were trying to do with your eyes the first time we met her," quipped Zack. "You too, Cash."

Both men looked at Zack with knowing faces.

"Like you all innocent. You should have seen the way you were watching her hips sway," said Cash.

"Okay, jokes aside, I do want her, but don't want to rush anything," said Zack.

Cash and Blaze nodded.

"Let's get back to trying to catch this damn stalker," said Zack as he looked around the table at the men. Zack went from jokes to commanding in two minutes flat.

"I can call a few of my friends in law enforcement," said Blaze, "to see what information I can get."

Blaze enjoyed guns and going to the shooting range. He had met several police officers there. Now, he held several charity events with them and helped out whenever he could.

"Blaze, that sounds like a plan," said Zack as he reached for his phone. "I'll call a few people who are running the streets."

Zack still had contacts from his days of underground fighting. He also still fought at the dojo legally. He offered boxing classes whenever he wasn't working.

"Cash, you check her contacts and see if anyone saw or knows anything."

Denise walked down the stairs. All eyes looked at her. Her long legs peeked from the thigh-high shorts. Her crop top showed her toned abs and full breast. Ringlets of curls pulled away from her high ponytail and framed the sides of her face.

She didn't feel shy about their perusal but welcomed the desire that she saw in their eyes.

"Denise, did you find everything you needed?" asked Zack.

"Yes, I have everything I need, except food," she said with a laugh.

"We ordered pizza from Domino's," said Blaze. "Come eat with us."

She noticed and liked the command coming from Blaze because people never told her what to do or eat.

Denise sat between Blaze and Zack. Her legs slightly touched Blaze as she sat at the table, sending a shimmer through her core. Blaze placed a slice of pepperoni pizza in front of Denise.

"Denise, we called contacts that we know to see what we can find out. But there wasn't any new information, only what you told us. The police are looking into tracking the phone calls to see if they can get some leads. Cash will need to know your contacts, so he can call to see if they know anything we may have missed."

"Thanks, guys. This has been unreal. I have never had anything happen like this before, and it's thrown me off." She rubbed her thighs and looked down. "I must admit that I do act like a diva, and maybe that's why this is happening."

The men looked at each other and then back at Denise. They didn't want her to feel guilty for what someone was doing to her.

"Yes, it could be the reason why, but no one should hurt anyone for the way they act. It doesn't give them the right," said Zack.

Denise looked sad and vulnerable. Zack leaned over to embrace Denise. He wanted to comfort her and take away her worries. He didn't know why, but the desire to protect her was strong.

"Denise, tell us about yourself and the people who are in your life. We can generate a list of possible suspects."

Denise was hesitant about revealing her true self.

"I... I..." said Denise.

"You can trust us," Zack said.

I grew up with my sister and grandmother after my parents were killed in a car accident."

"Sorry for your loss," said Zack as he took her hand and led her to the couch.

"After that, I went to college and then started acting. I had several boyfriends but nothing came of it. Most left because I didn't have the time to cultivate a relationship or because they couldn't deal with the limelight."

Cash sat on the other side of Denise and embraced her.

"But you still managed to make a name for yourself and become a star."

Denise liked the way Cash managed to find the good in situations.

"Yes, but no more talk about me. What about you guys?"

"You know we were in Afghanistan, but what we didn't mention is that we saw some stuff there that people should never see. A lot of deaths. It haunted us for a long time when we came back." Blaze opened his eyes as if he was still there. He looked like he had seen a ghost.

Zack moved to pat him on the back.

"But we made it," said Zack.

Zack continued, "We made it back, got some counseling, and now we are seriously looking for the missing piece in our family unit." Zack swiped his hand through his beard.

Denise looked at the floor. She didn't know if this was an outright statement that she was that missing piece or if it was just talking.

"I want to thank you for your service. Many people don't quite understand the sacrifice and courage it takes."

She stood and hugged Blaze. She pulled Zack and Cash into the hug as well. It felt right that she was there hugging these men. She felt completely safe.

Zack broke the silence. "Hey everyone, let's take a walk on the beach before the sun goes down. Because one, we need to work off the pizza we just ate, and two, it will help us all relax."

Zack looked at Denise. "Would you join us?"

"Of course, I will."

Zack led her by the hand through the glass doors and outside to the private beach. The breeze from the ocean felt warm on Denise's skin. She walked in the middle of the guys, talking, laughing, and stopping to admire seashells and sand dollars. Each guy took turns walking next to her. It wasn't planned but natural. One guy would hold her hand or another guy would pull her in for an embrace. Denise felt alive. She enjoyed the connection she felt with the men.

"The sun is about to set. Let's sit and watch as it goes down," Cash said.

Cash took off his shirt and placed it on the sand for Denise to sit. Denise stared at Cash's chest in appreciation. Zack sat to the left of Denise and Blaze sat behind Denise. She felt covered and safe.

The ocean waves roared as they licked the surface of the beach. A silverfish flashed beneath the waters. Denise breathed in the invigorating smells of sand and seaweed. The sun started to descend behind moving clouds.

"Can I kiss you?" whispered Cash in Denise's ear.

She gasped and looked at him. Denise had been propositioned many times, but none had captured her like the sincerity in Cash's voice. It was like he was holding his breath until she replied.

"Yes," said Denise, and she moved her head toward him.

Cash took her mouth slowly at first but couldn't hold back. He leaned forward, which caused her to lay back into the lap of Blaze. Blaze held her while Cash took the kiss deeper. She rubbed her fingers down Cash's chest towards his abs and downward. His groin began to tighten. He didn't know how far her hands would go down. Maybe she would stroke his cock. Maybe he would pull her little shorts down and fuck her in the sand with his brothers. His thoughts were everywhere with Denise.

As Denise was wrapped in the kiss and Blaze's arms, she let out a small moan which edged Cash deeper.

"Um, uh," Zack interrupted. "You are almost missing the sunset," he said with a smile. "Plus, I want a turn to kiss you."

He moved closer to Denise after she was released from Blaze's hold. He looked in the depth of her eyes and caressed her face with both hands. He knew she was a rising actress and didn't know how this would affect her career, so he paused and simply took in her beauty.

Denise had never been stared at like that before. It increased her anticipation of the kiss. Zack nibbled at Denise's just-kissed swollen lips. His brother did a good job making her moan, which turned him on. He was hard as steel, and he hadn't even fully kissed her yet.

But that would change now. He started by licking the edges of her mouth. Then he took her bottom lip in between his, sucking first then nibbling. After lingering on the outside of her mouth, he took her lips firmly. Denise closed her eyes to feel the sensations that mingled throughout her body. Her nipples ached and her core clenched. How could these two incredible men turn her inside and out with just a kiss?

Knowing that Blaze was probably waiting to taste Denise and that they both would need air, Zack released her from the kiss. She was starry-eyed and had a dazed expression as Blazed picked her up. She relaxed in his arms and leaned against his solid body.

He cradled Denise and kissed her with all the passion and restraint he had. She didn't back down as he plummeted her mouth with rigor. How could he be so firm but gentle at the same time? Denise was in awe of the strong man who held her tight while he drove her insane with lust. She was confident enough to flutter her tongue in his mouth so he could taste her sweet essence. They devoured each other's mouths as the other two brothers looked on.

At that moment, no one knew what was going on, but they were swept up in desire. The waves crashed against the beach, breaking the kiss.

"We should get back to the house. It's going to get dark soon," said Zack.

Blaze gently placed Denise on her feet. Her legs wobbled as her head was still spinning with lust. He held her hand to stabilize her and to be near her. They walked back to the house holding hands.

Denise entered the house with the guys following behind. Once everyone was inside, they circled Denise. It was like she had a wall of protection made of men. She wasn't shy and took to her position well.

"Thank you for helping me today," Denise said as she hugged each man. "The day started badly, but now with resting on the beach and more, I feel a lot better." She smiled with a glimmer in her eye. "I normally don't do that sort of thing in public, but with all of you, there is a connection. I don't understand it, but it is something to explore."

The men smiled. They were happy that she was open to exploring at least.

Blaze shoved his hands deep in his pockets to stop himself from grabbing another hug.

"Thanks, Denise, for allowing us to share a sweet moment and time at the beach," said Cash.

"Thanks, guys. It's getting late, so I'm going up to my room."

"Denise, thank you for letting us protect you and getting to know you better," said Zack. "Tomorrow we can call your contacts to see if we can find any leads. Our main priority is protecting you."

He leaned over and brushed a soft kiss on her cheek. The guys followed suit but kissed her on her forehead and the other cheek.

"Denise if you need anything, let us know. We will be right next to you," said Cash with a wicked smile.

"Thanks, Cash. I know you all are just a door's length away."

Denise walked upstairs, leaving the men to their own devices.

Chapter 7: Cash and Zack

Denise entered the room, walked over to the queen-sized platform bed, and slumped down. How in the world did she get to this point? Today had started okay, but it all got messed up with the threat to her life. She looked out the window into the night sky. Who would want to harm me, she wondered.

Her fingernails left imprints inside her hand from balling them into fists. She mentally went over a shortlist of names, but none stood out. She slowly released her hands. She was in the Keys with three hotter-than-hell men who had protected her and might want more. She saw the sexual hunger in their eyes, but she also thought she saw something else there too. Denise shook her head. Maybe they just wanted a fling, and maybe she needed one too. It had been way too long since anyone had touched her body, and it was aching for a release. The kisses that each man had rendered left her shaken to the core. Her pussy clenched at the thought of the men doing more than kissing.

What was it that made these men any different than the ones she normally messed with? Maybe it was the fact that being with all three had piqued her curiosity. She wondered what it would feel like to have their hands and mouths all over her. What it would be like to have Blaze fucking her from the back while she sucked Cash's and Zack's dicks. Denise ran her hand between her legs but didn't have access because of her jeans. She was more than sexually frustrated. Then she thought about what Zack had said when he mentioned that they were looking for a woman to love. Could it be more than just sex?

She didn't know if she had feelings for them because it was too early. She did know that she trusted and liked them. Each man had something different that interested her. She liked Cash for his sincerity. She liked Blaze for his gentleness, and she liked Zack for the way he took charge. She knew they weren't blood brothers but were bonded through their selfless service to the military. She thought about Blaze's broad shoulders and powerful legs that had carried her on the beach. He was gentle and treated her like a fragile flower. She liked the way Zack took control of the kiss and almost drove her to climax. She also liked the way Cash was always thinking about keeping her safe and protected. Denise stood and went to the bathroom. She turned on the shower and undressed as the water changed from cold to hot, and steam filled the room. She stepped in and let the warm water caress her skin. She continued thinking about the men. She didn't know what sharing herself would entail, but it was exciting to feel more than one man touching her while kissing. Plus, it was a relief that they weren't jealous of each other.

Thoughts ran through Denise's mind about the stalker and the men. She didn't know what to do about either. She turned off the water, towel blotted, and stepped from the shower. She then dressed in her two-piece red teddy and slipped into bed. She was still on edge as she tried to sleep. The images of the dead bird flickered in her mind. She tossed back and forth. She knew she wouldn't be able to sleep, so she got up from the bed and crept out the door toward downstairs. But before she could make it, Cash called her name.

"Denise. Denise, is everything all right?"

She turned to find a shirtless Cash standing in the doorway. She raked her gaze over his body appreciatively. His six-pack of muscles almost caused her to lose her breath. A thin trail of brown hair reached down past his navel and disappeared in his gray sweats.

OMG, thought Denise mentally.

After finally looking at his eyes, she spoke.

"Yes, everything is okay. I... I... just can't sleep." She folded her arms over her too tight nipples. "Everything that happened today is still racing through my head. This stalker shit is a trip. I've been trying to figure out who it could be, but no one comes to mind." She paused to think.

"Let's go downstairs and get a drink," said Cash. "I normally have a hard time sleeping too, but sometimes a drink helps."

Denise thought about it for a second and then replied, "I will take that drink, Cash. At this point, I will try just about anything to get some rest."

He walked from his doorway, took Denise's hand, and headed down the stairs to the kitchen. Denise sat at the bar while Cash rounded the counter to prepare the drinks.

Cash had seen Denise act in movies and knew she was good and had what it took to be an even bigger star, but he had read about her online after they had agreed to take the case and found out that she was a diva. She could be temperamental and difficult to please, but in real life, he saw something quite different. He saw a strong, independent lady who didn't take anything from anyone.

"How does a big movie star like yourself like your drink?" joked Cash.

"The same way most people like their drink," Denise said, "good and strong."

Cash and Denise laughed. The sexual current was evident with both. Cash handed Denise a glass of Jack and coke. Denise drank from it.

"This is good."

"You can't get Jack and coke wrong," teased Cash as he smiled at Denise and took a draw from his drink.

She noticed how his sweats hung low on his waist and his arm was wrapped in a tattoo of a lion. She observed how his tongue met the glass before his lips. She crossed her legs to quench the need that had arisen within her pussy. Denise took another sip of her drink to cool herself down more.

"Tell me your story," requested Denise.

She stared at the handsome man. She normally didn't go for the light-skinned pretty boys, but Cash was different. His full beard covering the lower part of his jaw gave him an almost regal look. His broad chest and masculine build caught her breath. Cash put the glass on the bar counter, which broke Denise from staring.

"Ma familia owns a large company that deals in mergers and acquisitions. They take failing small companies, buy them, and merge them into bigger companies. As I grew up, it was imparted to me that I would take over the business and that *la familia es primera*. Family is first."

Cash looked off in the distance. He ran his hand over his beard and nibbled at his bottom lip.

"But I wanted to go in a different direction. I wanted to have my own business, but it was hard getting started when everyone knew your family business. Plus, my family didn't understand why I didn't want to continue the legacy they had started. So, I joined the military. It was challenging being stationed overseas in the desert until I met *mis hermanos,* my brothers."

Denise came around the bar. She placed her arms around Cash. She squeezed gently and then he closed his eyes. She saw his vulnerable side as well as his strength. She placed her head against his shoulder as he pulled her closer. His woodsy smell permeated her senses. She inhaled to take in the intoxicating scent.

Zack, hearing something moving in the kitchen, got up from his bed. He wanted to make sure Denise was okay. Looking over the banister and down to the kitchen, he saw Denise and Cash talking. He didn't want to interrupt them from making a connection, so he would wait to spend time with Denise. He had feelings for her too and couldn't understand how they had developed so fast. Yes, she was beautiful, but she was more. There was a depth to her that he hadn't seen in someone before. Zack waited upstairs until he had the opportunity to be with Denise.

"Tell me something about yourself," said Cash as he stared down at the woman in his arms.

She was pretty but in a natural way. Her face shone with hues of browns and tans. Rich smells of shea butter and vanilla wafted in the air. He felt her full breast and taut nipples against his chest. His cock strained against his pants, begging for release. He pushed back the brown tendril that hung in her face to get a better look at her eyes. Denise was quiet for a moment. Cash continued to hold her. He wanted her to open up and share her life with him and them, but he didn't want to force it. He knew he wanted her from the moment they met. She stirred something in him that was different from any woman he had ever been with. It was sexual but much more. He had a deep desire to protect and care for her. At first, it shocked him that he would have such a deep connection so fast. Because he didn't want to be hurt, he took a wait-and-see approach.

Denise looked up with sadness in her eyes. He had seen it there before, but she had managed to push it away. But this time, it lingered. Cash wanted to protect her from the pain. Why did he feel this strongly about a woman he had just met?

"My sister and I grew up in a family with a lot of love. Our parents embodied what the word meant, but it all changed one night when they didn't come home. They had died in a car accident."

"I am so sorry," said Cash as he rubbed her back.

"We were then raised by our grandmother. She was a stern lady and didn't show us much love. My sister Jasmine was like the mother that I didn't have. This made us close."

"Denise, you've been through a lot, and now this thing with the stalker."

He leaned down to brush a comforting kiss on her lips, but the fire inside of them wanted more. His hands roamed her back and descended lower to cup her ass. Cash pulled from the kiss.

"I want you, *mi renia,* my queen."

"I want this too," said Denise.

He walked her to the couch and sat down at her feet.

"Let me do something for you."

Cash removed the bottom of her teddy.

"Spread your legs, Denise. I want to see you."

Denise's pussy glistened as Cash beheld the site. His dick hardened even more as he gazed upon the feast he was about to eat. He couldn't wait any longer. He slid his finger in her slit, pulled it out, and tasted her excitement. *Mi renia,* your pussy is soaking, and I want to taste you."

She was ready and so was he. His dick ached and pressed against his sweats.

"Yes," she breathlessly moaned.

He lowered his face, extended his tongue, and licked her wet folds. She tasted of honeycomb and nectar. He dipped his tongue into her cunt and she let out a whimper. Denise clenched the couch as he devoured her pussy. Licking and sucking, his tongue was all over her.

"Yes, yes," Denise moaned and closed her eyes.

"Look at me," demanded Cash. "I want to see your face when you come in my mouth." Their eyes locked on each other was just what Denise needed. She shook and shuddered her release into Cash's wicked mouth. He fingerfucked her as her cunt squeezed his digits. He sucked her clit until she gasped his name.

"Cash!"

Denise became boneless.

"Mi renia, you are so beautiful when you are coming. Turn over so I can make you come again."

Cash helped position Denise with her knees on the seat of the couch and her head on the back of the couch. Her ass was up in the air which gave Cash the perfect opportunity to taste her again.

"*Mi renia,* I can't get enough of your sweet pussy."

"Cash, I want it so bad," said Denise as she rocked her impatient ass against his hard-as-steel cock.

"I want you, too, but I must protect you first."

He grabbed a condom from the small drawer underneath the living room table. He pulled down his sweats and quickly sheathed himself. He kissed Denise up and down her back. He spoke to her in his native language. Denise felt cherished.

"Let me join in on the fun?" commanded Zack.

He had watched Cash fuck Denise with his tongue from upstairs, and his arousal stirred within. Hearing Denise moan clawed at his senses.

"Yes," said Denise as she looked at Zack.

Curiosity and arousal sparked her to have both guys pleasuring her at the same time.

Cash continued kissing Denise on her back. He toyed with her clit to ensure she was ready for him.

"Take off your shirt so I can get a taste of you," said Zack.

She took off her shirt, exposing her full globes. Zack knelt his head to flicker and nibble at her nipples. She arched her back and closed her eyes.

Cash kissed her shoulders and feather-kissed her down her back while Zack hungrily sucked her brown peaks. The men worked her with their mouths and hands, but she wanted more.

"Yes, yes, more. Please fuck me." She needed something to put out the ache between her legs.

"We'll take care of you, *Renia*."

Cash positioned his cock near her entrance and slid in deep. He wanted her to feel every inch of what he was feeling. He gave her a chance to adjust to his width before stroking her walls.

"Open your mouth so you can taste *mi hermano*," said Cash.

Denise opened her mouth and angled her head. Zack slowly pushed his long, thick dick inside. He softly held her as he rocked into her mouth.

"This feels so fucking good."

He watched as Cash took her from behind. Her ass bounced as he plowed into her. This propelled him to move even more. Denise grabbed Zack's cock with one hand and worked it back and forth with her mouth.

"Fuck! Fuck! Fuuuck! I won't last like this, said Zack."

She had to focus because Cash was pounding her pussy. This was exactly what she wanted and needed. Her orgasm grew. She had never felt anything so intense. She moaned loudly around Zack's cock.

"Cash, give her more," said Zack.

She thrust her ass backward to receive more of Cash's strokes. They moved together.

Zack released first inside of Denise's mouth. His cum spilled from her lips.

"Come for me," said Cash as he rubbed her clit and deeply thrust in and out.

Her senses were on fire. That's all it took for Denise to cry out her orgasm.

"Yessssssssss! Yes! Yes!"

Which brought Cash to his release as well. He tried to hold back his groin, but it erupted in spite of his attempt. He clung to her back and slowly moved inside of her as the last of his seed slipped from his body.

"*Renia,* you are amazing."

He kissed her neck as he withdrew from her vagina. He moved to throw away the condom and to give Zack a chance to sex their woman. Zack came around to the front of the couch with a new erection. Pulling her up to him, he kissed Denise. She kissed him back, stoking the flames of passion. Zack broke from the kiss and placed his head against hers.

"I want to be inside you so bad."

"I want you too," said Denise.

"Let's go to my room." said Zack.

Zack and Denise went upstairs with Cash following behind. They entered Zack's room with a California king bed. They laid Denise on the bed with her legs splayed open. She opened her legs further, and her dark curls parted to expose her pink feminine flesh.

"You are so beautiful," said Zack.

He looked Denise in the eyes.

"There is a side of me that I want you to know about. I have a need to dominate, to be in control, in the bedroom. It shouldn't scare you, but I like to push the limits. Do you trust me?"

Denise had heard about dominance and submission but had never experienced it. She trusted Zack and knew in her heart that he wouldn't hurt her. Cash go to the top of the bed to hold Denise, commanded Zack.

"Denise, we like the way you give yourself to both of us," said Zack. "If you were ours, you would want for nothing sexual or otherwise."

Zack bent to lick Denise's pussy.

"You taste so damn good. Now I see why Cash spent so much time with his tongue inside of you."

"Yes, yes. Mm-hmm," she moaned and arched her hips up.

"Zack it feels so good," said Denise.

Denise held Zack's head in place while he fucked her with his tongue. Thrusting in and out of her entrance, he savored the taste of her as her juices filled his mouth. Cash rubbed her mounds while he lavished kisses on her shoulders and neck.

Zack wanted to make it good for Denise, but he couldn't wait to plunge inside of her. With one hand, he opened the drawer on the nightstand and fished out a condom. He quickly covered himself. Next, he lifted both her legs over his shoulders and thrust his long, thick dick deep inside, hitting her G spot. Denise screamed out in ecstasy. Her face contorted.

"Fuuuuuuuck!!"

Cash covered her mouth with his, then released her.

"*Renia*, we don't want to wake Blaze. He's a bit of a grizzly bear when he wakes up." Cash smiled at Denise while she was upside down.

Zack continued to thrust deeper and deeper into Denise's wet cunt.

"She's so fucking tight and wet," said Zack.

Denise started moaning louder. Denise don't cum until I tell you to. Your orgasm belongs to Cash and I.

"Cash, stick your dick in her mouth," commanded Zack.

He did, not to keep her quiet, but because he couldn't resist having her lips on him. Cash dipped his cock deeper and deeper into Denise's mouth. He eased up a little so she could breathe.

Denise started to shake as a tear of joy slipped from her eyes.

"Umm," moaned Denise. The pressure of the orgasm building fast and hard within.

She never thought that two men fucking her brains out would be this good.

Cum for us Denise, said Zack as he pumped into her core.

Her legs trembled, and when she couldn't hold back anymore, she gushed out her orgasm.

Feeling the grip on his dick, Zack exploded with a bang. Cash followed, spilling his cum on her lips and face.

Afterwards, Zack positioned Denise next to Cash and got up from the bed.

"Denise, thanks for being open to this. I know it's unconventional, but it can work. Let me clean you up."

Denise reached for his hand.

"Thank you for this experience." She saw the heat still radiating in his eyes.

He went to get a towel to clean her off.

"*Renia,* you were wonderful tonight. I hope we weren't too much," said Cash as he licked his lips.

"No, you both were amazing. I have never experienced anything like that before."

"*Renia*, we want to take care of you and more."

Denise wasn't sure what the "more" would entail but wanted to enjoy the night.

Zack came back with a warm towel and wiped Denise down.

"Thank you, Zack, for taking care of me."

"No problem. We take care of what we want."

Denise didn't want to think too much about what they were saying, but could there be more?

Eventually, she went to the bathroom to clean up. In the bathroom, she looked at herself in the mirror. She looked thoroughly fucked but happy. She wondered, with two, it was mind-blowing, but what would be like having all three even if it was for a short time? After putting her hair in a ponytail and splashing her face with water, she went back to aroused, waiting men. She couldn't believe they were ready for her again, but she enjoyed being wanted.

Denise didn't stay clean for long. They worked her pussy throughout the night. When one was finished, the other took his place. Kissing, sucking, fucking, talking, and doing whatever to please Denise.

Denise's mind was blown. She had never felt so utterly fulfilled. The guys pleasured her beyond anything she had experienced. But it was more than that. They had given and taken but made her feel comfortable, wanted, and needed. As the night turned to dawn, they fell asleep with Denise entwined between them.

Chapter 8: Blaze

Denise woke early the next morning with Zack's arm around her waist and Cash molded to her back. The night had been better than anything that she had ever experienced. The men touched parts of her that had been dormant for years. They had awakened her senses and her needs. She couldn't believe she was getting aroused again after all the sex that she had last night. Gently, she slid from underneath Zack's arm and quietly got out of bed. She tiptoed out of the room and went downstairs. She grabbed her phone to call Jasmine. She needed to talk with her sister

"Jasmine, are you awake?"

"Yes, now I am," said a drowsy Jasmine.

"Is everything okay, Denise?"

"Yes."

"Okay, Denise, talk. I have been worried about you all night. After the incident that happened yesterday, I couldn't stop thinking about you."

"It's going better than good. The men treat me like a queen. They are kind and have been protecting me."

"Denise, it sounds like there's more than what you're telling me."

"Last night, we were together."

"What? How? Who?!"

"First, Cash and I had a connection that led to more, and then Zack joined us. It was an out-of-body experience."

"So, you slept with both the men. Were they upset?"

"Oh, no. I slept with them at the same time."

"Denise, what the hell is going on?"

"Oh, I didn't tell you, but they share women. They're looking for a woman that they all can love. It's like your relationship."

Jasmine was speechless. She covered her mouth. She didn't know if she should be happy or sad for her sister.

"Denise, do you want this type of relationship? It can be a lot sometimes, dealing with the different personalities and needs of each man."

"I didn't think about that part, and I'm not sure what I want. I thought I wanted a fling, but I feel like there could be more."

"Be careful with your heart, sister. I don't want to see you get hurt."

"Thanks for the advice, big sis."

"You know I am here for you. Now, what's going on with the stalker? Have there been any more calls or any incidents since you arrived in Key West?"

"No, there haven't been any calls or incidents. It's been quiet lately."

"Keep on your guard and stay vigilant."

"Yes, you know I will. No worries. The men and I got this."

"Okay."

"Talk to you later."

"Bye."

Denise and Jasmine hung up the phone. The phone started ringing again. Thinking it was Jasmine, Denise answered.

"Hey, Jasmine, what did you forget?"

The auto-tuned voice felt like a knife piercing Denise's ear.

"I know where you work and where you live. I am going to kill you, Denise. If I can't have you, no one else will!"

"Who is this?" screamed Denise.

The phone went silent.

Hearing Denise scream, Blaze ran downstairs.

"Denise, is everything okay?"

He picked her up and cradled her in his arms. She was trembling all over and was in shock.

"Talk to me, Denise."

"It... it was the stalker."

Blaze placed Denise on the couch and grabbed her phone. He fiercely scrolled through it looking for the number.

"It's always anonymous."

"We have to stop the bastard. He can't get away with this."

Blaze radiated with anger. He looked down at the phone like it should be murdered but handed it back to Denise. She took the phone and placed it on the table face down.

"I am so sorry, Denise. Please know we will catch whoever is playing these sick games and make them pay."

Blaze sat next to Denise. He rubbed her shoulder to comfort her.

"I know you all will find them."

She leaned over to hug Blaze. Blaze held her as he gently caressed her hair. He wanted to take her pain away.

Breaking from the hug, he suggested, "Let's get out of here. A walk along the beach will do us some good."

He grabbed a beach blanket before leaving so they could sit and talk.

The sun was about to peek over the clouds. The morning air was crisp. Denise and Blaze strolled mutually silently along the beach. Denise looked at the stocky pounds of power walking beside her. His bald head and bearded face made him look like a bodybuilder. Muscles rippled down his toned legs. His armed flexed with every movement. She was captivated. But so was he. He looked at her like she was a prize.

"Blaze, tell me something about you."

Blaze was the quiet one of the group but his large presence was felt by all.

"Denise, I want to open up to you more, but it's hard. I'm not used to talking about my feelings, but I will try."

He was quiet for a minute before he spoke.

"I have been through so much in the past." He shook his head as if to shake the demons of the past away.

"Was it during your time in the military?"

"Yes, but for most of my life, it has been rough. I grew up in the streets, and military life saved me. But being in the military changes you as a person. I can remember being in Afghanistan. There was a lot of death there. Once, when we were on patrol around the perimeter of our camp, we rolled over and detonated a land mine. Everyone was hurt, but one of our troops didn't make it. We tried to save him, but it was too late. His injuries were too extensive. We were all hurt too. He was part of our unit. For a long time, I couldn't shake the image of his face from my mind. The helplessness and guilt were all I felt.

Blaze looked down at the sand. It was like he was looking at an image. Denise grabbed his hand, hoping to pull him from the terrible dream he was having."

"Blaze, what are you thinking?"

"I could have done more."

"You were injured too. It wasn't your fault."

Blaze looked at the woman near him. He needed to hear those words. He pulled her to him.

"Thank you, Denise. I know it was a long time ago, but sometimes it's hard to shake. I have been to counseling, and it's helped. But sometimes, I regress, and when I do, my brothers are there to help me get back to a good place."

Denise looked at the gentle giant with so much hurt and pain. She wanted to take away his pain. She reached up and kissed him. She conveyed with the kiss that things would be okay.

Blaze was elated that Denise had kissed him. He had been thinking about doing it again all night. He kissed her back with as much passion as he had inside. His hand roamed over her ass and hips. He liked the way she felt. She was soft in all the right places. Then Blaze broke from the kiss. He took the blanket and spread it over the white sand. He took Denise's hand and helped her sit on the blanket.

"Denise, tell me something about yourself."

"I went through a lot growing up without parents, but my sister was there for me. I think, in some way, she helped me to be the person I am today. To a certain extent. Not the diva part," laughed Denise. "Sometimes, I play this role of being a diva as a way to protect myself."

"I understand," said Blaze. "It's hard trusting people, but sometimes we have to break down the walls and let people in."

Denise shivered under the cool morning air and at the words that Blaze had said.

"Come closer," said Blaze in his baritone voice. "I can keep you warm."

Denise stood and straddled Blaze.

"Is this close enough?" Her body begged for his touch.

"Denise, do you know what you are doing?"

"Yes, I know what I want and what I am doing."

He liked her brazenness.

She undulated her hips on top of his swollen groin. He unwillingly let out a moan.

"I don't think you know what you're doing to me."

Blaze looked at the gorgeous lady on top of him, and his breath caught. Her brown eyes flared wide, and her irises locked on his. He inhaled the sand mixed with her scents of vanilla.

"I don't want to move too fast with you, Denise, but I am losing my restraint."

Desire radiated between them. Her flesh tingled with anticipation.

Every inch of him craved her. He took her mouth firm and fast. Heat coursed through his veins. He thrust up as she undulated her hips.

Longing whispered through her.

"I want this," she said, placing her head against Blaze. "*I need...*"

She slowly stood up, removed her top, and slid her bottoms down her legs.

He gasped as he looked up at the woman standing in front of him. Fucking beautiful Denise.

"Come here."

He took off his clothes. His dark brown skin glistened. His powerful build sent a quiver through Denise's core. He fisted his erection, stroking it to let her see what he was working with.

She straddled him but didn't get on his python of a dick. She thought about it, and she realized she hadn't been with anyone this big before. As she sat atop him, his dick reached past her stomach. She wasn't scared, but she was taken aback at how large and long he was. She wasn't sure she could accommodate him. He saw the concerned look in her eye and smiled.

"It will fit. We will make it work."

His body throbbed for her. He lifted her on her knees to stroke her clit. She looked into his eyes, and they brimmed with passion and pleasure. He lifted her higher so his mouth could tongue her entrance. He levitated her up and down on his mouth like she was weightless, swirling his tongue in and out of her cunt.

"Yes, yes!" yelled Denise.

Her juices ran down his chin.

"You are so fucking wet."

Passion took hold of him as he sucked the nub into his mouth.

"I want you to come for me, baby."

He slid his finger up and penetrated her walls while he balanced her with his hand. He stroked a burning fire that grew in intensity.

She exploded in a downpour of fiery sensations as she moaned loudly and shouted his name.

"Blaze! Blaze!"

Pulling her down from the air, he sat her atop his lap. He pressed his lips to her.

"I like the way you taste, but I can't wait to fuck that pussy."

He showered her with more kisses around her lips and neck. His dick throbbed against her stomach, begging her to let him in. Gaining confidence, she lifted herself and aligned her opening to his dick.

"Take your time, I don't want to hurt you."

His lips teased a taut brown nipple.

"I want you so bad," said Blaze.

"I want you too."

His hands moved gently down the length of her back. In one forward movement, she took the bulb of his head into her walls.

The stretch.

The burn.

The pleasure. Oh, the pleasure.

She gasped as she lowered her body down on the wood stock. She continued to use her weight to take more of his length.

"Damn, you are so fucking tight."

"Damn, you are so fucking big," said Denise as she moaned in pain and pleasure.

"Ummm! Ummm!"

She felt her walls stretching to accommodate the intrusion.

"Let me help you, baby."

His urgency grew to explosive proportions.

He pushed the rest inside and waited while she adjusted.

"Baby, I have to move or I am going to bust."

As he moved inside her, she clawed at his back and bit his shoulder.

"Fuck! Fuck! Fuck!"

Sweat beaded on Blaze's head.

"Yes! Yes! Yes!"

"I'm about to come!" yelled Denise as he pumped her from the bottom.

She undulated her hips. She was filled to the hilt with his cock, but she wanted more.

She rode him fast and hard. Together they found the rapid tempo that bound their bodies together.

"You're so fucking tight and wet, Denise."

Blaze rolled over with Denise underneath. He pressed his hard body against her soft curves. He thrust his hips and pumped her faster. Her legs shook as her orgasm built like a freight train speeding ahead. The hot tide of passion raged through them as they released together, moaning each other's name.

"Blaze!"

"Denise!"

She clung to him as he cradled her in his arms. It felt like forever.

"Denise, I have never felt anything so damn good."

"It was so good," said Denise with a sated smile.

He kissed her, devouring her lips.

"Are you trying to go for another round?" asked Denise.

The smile in his eyes contained a sensuous flame.

"Yes, if I can."

"You're such a bad boy."

"Let's go. We still have to find that damn stalker."

Blaze and Denise stood up and dusted the sand from their skin. Needing to cool down, Blaze took off running and jumped in the ocean, ass and all showing.

Not wanting to be left, Denise quickly moved after him and splashed in as well. She was sore, but the saltwater helped. They swam and kissed before returning to the house.

Chapter 9: United Front

Denise went inside the house with Blaze.

The guys standing in the kitchen stopped talking when they entered.

"Denise, you look like you have been set on fire," said Zack with a smile on his face.

"Yes, Blaze and I have connected," said Denise as a smile touched the corner of her lips.

Blaze kissed Denise and went to the sink to wash the sand from his hands.

"It's pretty cool that you guys don't have any qualms about me being with you all, but I feel a bit hesitant at times."

"You shouldn't," said Zack. "We just want you to be happy." He bent to kiss her.

Cash hugged her from the back and placed a kiss on her neck.

"If you are not too tired, we can go over your contacts. Afterward, we would love to take you to dinner."

"Hmm," said Denise. "That sounds like a plan. But I think you guys did it backward. First the date then the sex."

Blaze erupted with a deep baritone laugh along with his brothers. They talked and bantered back and forth, never leaving Denise out of the conversation.

Denise told the guys about the stalker calling earlier and mentioned that the person spoke, but their voice was auto-tuned. She listed her contacts while Zack took notes. He gave the list to Blaze.

Blaze took a picture of the list with his phone and then sent it to a cop that he knew. The cop mentioned that he would run the list through the criminal database and would call back. It would take a few days, but he would find something if there was something to be found.

"I am going to change for our date," said Denise.

"Take your time. We have to get ready as well," said Zack.

Denise went upstairs, leaving the men to talk.

The men sat around the table.

"Denise is fucking amazing," said Blaze. "She's strong-minded and bold. Hell, see how she handles our asses."

"I know, right? She could be the missing piece to our family," said Zack as he looked around the table at the men. "I have never felt anything like this with any other woman and so fast."

The men nodded in agreement.

"Not only is she sexy, but she cares about others," said Cash. "I don't see the diva that people in the media say she is. She has been through a lot, and the pain has built a hard exterior, but that is to be expected. I just don't want us to hurt her by not being there when she needs us."

"I agree," said Zack. "How about we ask her to be in a relationship with us? I know it's early to be asking, but I want her to know we are serious about her, and our feelings are genuine and real."

"I'm ready to take that step," said Cash.

"I am too," said Blaze with a smile that lit up his eyes.

"Let's ask during dinner. I know she has a lot going on with the stalker and her career, but we just want to ensure she is protected and see if we can build a future with her."

Chapter 10: At the Restaurant

Later that night, Blaze, Cash, Zack, and Denise walked to the restaurant near the beach house.

Inside Loggerhead Beach Restaurant, waiters moved from table to table to serve the needs of their guests. The band played reggae music as dancers swayed back and forth. The decor of seashells, driftwood, and glass containers lined the walls. Candle lights sitting on each table elicited a soft glow to set the mood. Views of the ocean could be seen from any table in the restaurant through the open patio doors. Outside, people lounged on the beach as they took in the display of the full moon and drank cocktails by twinkling string lights.

"Denise, thank you for joining us for dinner," said Zack as he stared into the most beautiful brown eyes he had ever seen. Her white linen see-through dress showed her delicate curves and the tiny two-piece coral bikini underneath.

"Thank you for the invite," said Denise as she gazed around at the gorgeous men.

Their skins reflected hues of light and dark browns from underneath tank tops held by broad muscular shoulders. Cargo shorts rode below sculpted abs. She was hooked. Not only did she like the way they looked, tasted, and smelled, she liked their inner being.

They dined on lobster tails and cheesy grits while drinking wine and rum.

"Denise, we brought you here for a reason," said Zack.

The look on his face was a little reserved, which caused Denise to sit back in her seat. He took her hand. Her pulse drummed loudly in her ear.

"There is nothing to worry about," Zack said. He paused, gathering his thoughts. "You know we like you."

"Yes," said Denise.

"We have feelings for you, and we want to see where this will lead. We want to ask you to be in a relationship with us. We know it's only been a couple of days, but to us, it feels like it's been years."

"We want you," said, Cash. "We haven't found anyone who has a connection with all of us, but you do, *Renia*. We like your boldness as well as your kind-heartedness when you choose to show it."

Blaze chimed in, "We know you've been through a lot, but we want you to take a chance, baby."

They pleaded with their eyes and hearts.

She leaned back in the booth and closed her eyes to think. Was this something that she wanted? Was this something that she could do?

Her thoughts raced through her mind, but one thing was constant. She trusted them.

"Denise, is everything okay?"

"Yes, I was just thinking."

"And....."

"I want to be in a relationship with you all too," she said as excitement raced through her.

She trusted them all and knew that they would protect her. She had feelings for them and wanted to see where things led.

Zack leaned in to kiss her long and hard, followed by Cash, who took her breath away with his feather-light kisses. Blaze picked her up and swung her around as he kissed her full lips. The people in the restaurant looked on in confusion. They didn't understand why she would be kissing all three guys so thoroughly.

"So, what does a relationship with all of you entail?" asked Denise with a scandalous look in her eye.

"That means that you are ours equally. We can have you anytime, and you can have any one of us anytime you want. We take care of your needs, and you take care of our needs. We get to know you on all levels."

"That sounds great," said Denise.

"*Nuestra reina*, I need something now," said Cash as he gazed into her eyes and then bent to nibble at her lips.

"What is it?" asked Denise.

"This," said Cash.

He moved his mouth over hers, devouring its softness. He took her lips possessively as he explored her mouth by nibbling and sucking. Her lips opened with his thrusting tongue. His tongue caused shivers of desire to race through her, and she gave herself freely to him.

She kissed him back, lingering and savoring every moment.

Zack's fingers slid sensuously up and down her soft legs as he kissed her neck. His groin tightened at the thought of being with her. His need drove him to touch her core. He parted her legs and moved her bikini to the side and dipped his finger deep in her wet slit. She moaned loudly through Cash's kiss. Cash pulled from the kiss at the sound of the loud moan and looked at the flustered expression on Denise's face.

"*Reina,* we love turning you on and getting you hot, but please moan lower as we don't want to bring too much more attention to our table." He smiled at her and continued his assault on her lips.

Blaze reached out and laced his fingers with hers, needing to touch her as he stroked himself through his shorts.

Zack drew circles around her swollen clit.

He whispered to her, "I want you to come, Denise but try not to make too much noise."

Zack worked her pussy with his finger. Deeper and deeper, he pushed inside. Her juice coated his digits. He moved them back and forth. He sucked fiercely at her neck, leaving a small mark. Denise's legs shook and trembled. Cash continued to kiss her, taking her breath away. Her mind began to swirl as Cash kissed her and Zack finger fucked her senseless. With his other hand, Zack pinched her nipple through her dress, which sent Denise over the edge of ecstasy.

She arched her back, bucked, and shook, but she never made a sound.

"That's our girl," said Zack as he licked her juices from his finger.

"I think we have made a spectacle of ourselves," said Cash as he looked around at the gawking guests who had a sense that something naughty was going on.

"Let's go," said Blaze with his huge erection visible through his shorts. "I want a chance to celebrate too and don't think I can wait until we get to the house."

"You won't have to wait," said Denise. "There were plenty of secluded areas along the way here."

Blaze reached out and caught her hand as he smiled and was happy to know that Denise was as adventurous as them.

"You still might have to wait, Blaze. I want first with Denise," said Cash as he ran his hand down his beard while licking his lips and looking at Denise.

"Don't leave me out," said Zack as he moved to hold Denise around her waist.

"Okay, guys, let's get out of here first. We're starting to get some weird stares," said

Denise, "and I want to be able to eat here again."

They paid the bill left the restaurant.

Chapter 11: Boardwalk

They walked along the path to enter the boardwalk, kissing and touching Denise.

"Here's a good place," said Zack as they reached a secluded area on the boardwalk.

Denise bent over the railing and arched her back. She parted her long slender legs. Cash got behind her, unzipped his cargo shirts, and lifted the little white dress. Blaze stood in front of her with his shorts unzipped and his dick out. Zack shifted to block the view of the boardwalk and Denise. He made sure no one was coming.

"Are you okay with this, Denise?"

"I am more than okay," said Denise as she wiggled her ass.

She bent her knees further for easy access.

With gentle fingers, Cash opened her pussy and drove into her with his dick to the hilt.

"Fuuuuuuck," he hissed as he bit down on his bottom lip. "You're so fucking wet."

Denise grabbed Blaze's big long dick and began sucking, while Cash pumped away at her pussy.

Leaning over, he whispered in her ear, "Suck his dick good, Denise."

He watched her mouth stretched over Blaze's cock. This sent him reeling to see his friend receive pleasure.

She writhed and moved as he whispered naughty words to her.

"Uhm hmm," she said with her mouth full.

"He gripped her hips and plowed deeper into her core.

"I am about to come," said Denise.

"So am I," said Cash.

Little cries and whimpers of ecstasy rang from Denise's mouth. Wave after wave crashed as they released in unison. Denise continued to work Blaze with her hand and mouth. Blaze jetted off like a rocket, squirting long streams of white-hot cum over Denise's face. Being able to half-watch was enjoyable for Zack. The thrill of not getting caught was exciting within itself.

"Hey, everyone, we should go. I see a couple coming down the boardwalk, and they may want to use our secret area," said Zack.

Blaze took off his shirt and wiped the cum from Denise's face. She enjoyed the view of his abs as they walked back to the beach house along the boardwalk. The current of need and sexual arousal blanketed the air.

Zack held Denise's hand, and Cash had her other hand as they walked to the beach house.

Chapter 12: Full Moon

After a short walk, they reached the beach house.

"Guys, thank you for the amazing night."

"But it's not over yet," said Zack. "Let's have some drinks and go for a night swim in our pool."

"Great idea," said Denise. "I already have a swimsuit on. Plus, it's beautiful outside with the full moon."

"You know what they say about the full moon," said Blaze.

"What?"

"People do all kinds of crazy things when the full moon is out."

"I hope that's true," Denise challenged.

"Blaze, man, you are too much," said Zack.

"So true," said Cash as he went to the kitchen to make drinks while Zack, Blaze, and Denise headed to the pool.

The waters of the pool glistened with the reflection of the moon. Crickets chirped in the distance. The full moon hovered close to the ground.

"It's such a beautiful night," said Denise.

"Not as beautiful as you," said Zack as he looked in her eyes and stroked her face.

"Thank you," said Denise. "I could not have imagined in a million years being with three great men. To think, I didn't have one man," she said with a laugh.

"Denise we're happy that you said yes to us and this unconventional relationship," said Zack.

"How in the world did we get a movie star to be our lady?" Blaze said as he ran his fingers down her face.

"I don't really know where this will lead," said Denise, "but I really just want to enjoy the moment and time together."

Zack stepped in between Denise's legs. He stood a good two inches over her and his body almost dwarfed her small frame.

"Thanks for giving us a chance. I know that it might be challenging, but we want to make this work."

He kissed her hungrily while his brother watched.

"I want you so bad," he said in between kissing.

He wrapped his arms around her waist as they took time to revel in the moment. Zack took the kiss deeper. He poured everything he had into it.

Denise let out a moan. She felt her mind spinning and her arousal growing. She also felt Cash kissing her shoulder and Blaze caressing her legs. She didn't know how she got to this moment of feeling so greedy for all of them, but she didn't want to let go of the feeling.

Zack rubbed his rigid dick up and down, letting Denise know how much he really wanted her.

"Denise, take off your swimsuit."

Denise untied the strings that held her top together. Her round globes with hard nipples floated on top of the water. She moved to shallow waters.

The men looked on, ready for a taste. Then she bent to take off her bottoms.

"Stay like that," said Zack.

Denise felt vulnerable bent over with her ass in the air as water splashed her pussy.

"Denise, do you trust us?"

"Yes."

"You know we won't do anything to hurt you, right?"

"Yes."

"Good."

Zack positioned himself behind Denise.

"Cash, stand in front of Denise and let her suck your dick," said Zack.

She released Cash's dick from his swim pants and immediately sucked it to the back of her throat. He moaned and leaned back onto the side of the pool. He braced himself as she worked his cock with her mouth.

"That's it, Denise, take him deep."

She was sandwiched between two men who could do anything to her, but she trusted them and knew that they only wanted her enjoyment and pleasure.

Zack pulled his cock out of his trunks and stroked it to harden even more. He bent to lick Denise from the back. She writhed and moved but couldn't go anywhere because she had Cash's cock in her mouth. He penetrated her with his tongue causing her to moan around Cash's cock. Blaze kissed her up and down her back.

"Denise, suck Blaze's dick. He looks like he wants some too," said Zack.

The intimacy was real. There was a connection that she couldn't explain. She continued to focus on sucking Cash's dick and leaned over to do the same to Blaze.

Seeing his brothers enjoying Denise aroused a strong passion and need. His dick hardened, and the precum started to leak.

"Denise, open your legs."

Denise's shifted to open her legs.

Zack spread Denise open and buried himself deep within her thighs.

"Fuckkkkk! Denise, you feel so fucking good."

He moved with purpose, back and forth. He wanted her to feel everything, so he kneaded her tits as he plunged into her core. It had been a while since they had a woman to share. Sherry was the last woman they had. She was a freak, but the connection wasn't there.

She would do anything they wanted, but mentally, it just didn't work. Now with Denise, the physical and mental connection was there and so fast.

Denise's loud moans brought Zack back to the reality of what they were doing. He increased his pace and pounded her deeper and harder. His brothers felt the impact as Denise sucked them in deeper and deeper down her throat. Taking Denise's head in his head, Blaze fucked her mouth.

"I'm about to come," said Blaze.

"Denise, come first," said Zack.

Denise didn't pull back because she wanted it as much as he did.

Cash moved his hand to rub Denise's clit. He could feel his brother moving inside of her.

"Holy shit," said Denise.

Her eyes fluttered closed as she erupted. Her body arched and her legs stiffened. She felt like hot molten lava on the inside, which caused Zack to plummet her pussy. He drove into her over and over until he growled his release over Denise's back. Denise stood up and moved closer to Cash, where she straddled his cock. He lifted and entered her with one swoop. She was wet and slick with the water from the pool and his friend's cum. He had to fill her with his now. She moved up and down on his rigid cock as Blaze kissed her from behind and Zack kissed her on the shoulders.

"You are so fucking amazing, *Renia*."

Denise and Cash moved at a rapid pace which caused the pool water to lightly splash around them.

"Come for me, *Renia*."

"Yes, yes."

He sucked her breast and fucked her cunt while Blaze penetrated her ass with his tongue.

"Holy shit!" Denise, feeling all the sensation, screamed her release.

Cash felt Denise's pussy gripping his cock and had to bust as well.

Blaze bent Denise over the side of the pool and entered her swiftly. He waited before he moved so Denise could adjust to his size and width.

Denise was almost delirious with the amount of cock and pleasure she was getting. She couldn't believe how fast and much the connection with the men had grown. These few days had felt like years.

Denise felt Cash kissing her mouth and Blaze's rock-hard dick fucking her into a new day.

"Yes, yes," she said in between the kisses.

Blaze's dick got even harder and stretched her pussy. She felt so tight around his cock. Blaze's fingers squeezed her soft ass as he filled her with his seed.

"Fuck, fuck, fuck," said Blaze as he fucked Denise into a hard, long climax.

A small tear of joy popped from Denise's eye. Her world had been shattered but in a good way.

The men poured their hearts and souls into her, but could she be everything they needed her to be? She had a career and a life. How would this work in the real world, she wondered?

Cash, seeing Denise in a daze, kissed her back to the present.

"Denise, you were fucking amazing," said Cash.

"So open and wet for us," said Zack.

"So sweet," said Blaze as he picked her up and carried her out of the pool to the large guest bedroom with the bathroom hidden away on the first floor.

Zack brought a towel to dry her off.

"You are were amazing too," said Denise. "It was such an outer-body moment."

Blaze placed her in the shower that Cash had turned on to warm.

"This feels good," said Denise.

"After what we just did, we figured we could all use a shower."

Blaze stepped behind Denise while Zack and Cash covered her front. They lathered her with soap, massaging and caressing her tender spots.

"You know, I was just getting started," said Denise with a sexy grin on her face.

"We must have turned you on with all of this washing we are doing," said Blaze.

Denise laughed, "I can't help that I am a greedy witch for all of you."

At the same time, Zack bent to his knees to lick his way down to Denise's center.

"Cash, open her pussy lips," said Zack as he worked his mouth over her clit.

Blaze slid his cock up and down between her cheeks. He felt her shake as he pushed the tip of it in her ass.

She gasped in sweet agony.

"It's okay, baby, I won't hurt you."

Cash kissed her hard to take her mind off of what Blaze was doing. She couldn't believe they were willing and able to go another round with her. Blaze pushed a little deeper into the too-tight place. Working it more and more caused him to lose his shit and release.

Denise straddled Zack's face and rode to a wave of ecstasy while Blaze pulled his cock from her ass leaving a trail of cum behind. Zack stood and kissed Denise.

"You taste so damn good."

He kissed her more as the water rained down on their heads. He slid his finger between the junction of her legs. She was still wet.

Removing his finger, he replaced it with his cock. Cash kissed her lightly on her shoulders.

"I want to be inside of you too."

She felt light-headed at the thought of being double penetrated.

Cash placed his cockhead at the junction of her thighs. Denise started to shake.

"It's okay, *Renia*. I won't hurt you."

He pressed deeper inside.

She moaned out of pleasure and a twinge of pain. Cash and Zack worked Denise's pussy and ass while Blaze watched and stroked his cock. Seeing his woman being pleasured by his brothers aroused his senses.

Denise moaned between kisses as they worked her from the front and the back. Their tempo increased as the passion swelled within Denise and the men. Her moans grew louder. Explosive currents raced through her. She shattered into a million pieces but somehow felt complete. She felt whole. Then the men erupted with groans of pleasure.

After kissing, they lathered Denise down again, but this time they rinsed and dried her. They all slept in the same bed with Denise in the middle and Zack at the head of the bed, with Cash and Blaze on each side. They were the perfect wall of protection.

Chapter 13: Crazy in Love

Over the next few days, Denise started to settle in. The guys made sure she had everything She needed. They took long walks on the beach and swam in the warm waters of the Gulf. They talked nonstop.

Getting to know each man excited her and took her mind off her current situation. While she was there, she helped Zack lead a youth boxing camp that helped inner-city children learn to use boxing as a way to manage anger. She and Cash spent time helping out at the homeless shelter. She loved his heart for people. Blaze showed her all about gun safety and how to hold a gun. Plus, the sex was always mind-blowing and pushed her out of her comfort zone. The stalker hadn't called, and everything seemed like it was okay.

Zack and Cash had left to get food and Blaze was at the police station checking on Denise's contacts. She was resting on the couch reading the book *The Power of Acting*.

Her phone rang, and she answered it. The auto-tuned voice echoed in her head.

"You are fucking them all. What a nasty bitch. I will make you and them pay."

"No, no!" screamed Denise as she pushed the end call button. Her hands trembled as she placed the phone down. Fear clawed through her.

How in the hell did the stalker know where she was and who she was with? He must be watching her. This shook her to the core. The guys were gone and, at the moment, that was a good thing. She needed to get out of there before the stalker hurt the men. She could take care of herself. She had done it before. She picked up her phone and called a LUber. Afterward, she went upstairs and packed what few clothes she had brought. She didn't want to leave the men because she had genuine feelings for them, but she couldn't risk the chance of them getting hurt or killed on account of her. She pulled out a pen and paper from her bag and scribbled a note: *This isn't working.*

Her phone chimed, alerting her that the LUber was out front. She placed the note on the table in the living room and left. She got into the black car with tinted windows.

What a shit show, she thought as she started the long ride back to Miami.

"Is everything all right?" asked the LUber driver looking through the vanity at the lady with the oversized shades.

"Yes, it's okay," said Denise with a small voice.

"This is going to be a long ride, but I will make it interesting," said the tall driver. "Would you like to listen to music?"

"No," said Denise. "I have a lot of stuff that I need to think about."

"Like what," asked the probing driver.

"It's personal," said Denise, trying not to be rude even though she was upset and angry.

She noticed how the men were always considerate and kind even in tough situations, and she wanted to turn over a new leaf and do the same.

"I have some personal stuff going on too," said the driver.

"Oh?" said Denise as she looked at the driver with the menacing eyes.

"I liked this lady a lot, but she won't give me the time of day."

Denise's blood ran cold as fear paralyzed her.

"And now she is all mine!" screamed the deranged driver.

Denise was trapped. She tried to open the door, but there weren't any handles on the inside of the car. She clawed at the door panels.

"Let me go!" she screamed.

"Fuck, no! I got you now. I've been waiting to make my move on you for a while. I watched you on the set of the movie. I watched you at that fancy apartment. I even watched you fuck those men. But now it's my turn."

He accelerated the car to 80, then 90 miles, and weaved in and out of the lanes.

"Please, please, slow down," said Denise.

Her pulse raced. How could she get out of the car?

"I got a little place where we can get acquainted, and don't even think about fighting back or calling anyone. I have already blocked your phone while I had it tapped."

The driver reached under the front passenger seat and pulled out the black Glock.

"Don't make me use this," he threatened, showing it to a visibly shaken Denise.

He slowed the car and pulled off the highway.

"What are you doing?"

"Be quiet, bitch!" he screamed as he exited the car with the gun in his hand.

He opened the door to where Denise was sitting. She tried to fight him but he knocked her out cold with the gun. He tied her arms and legs and laid her across the back seat and continued to drive to their final destination while singing along with his favorite song "Crazy in Love" by Beyoncé.

Chapter 14: This Isn't Working

This isn't working.

The men looked at the note lying on the table.

"How the fuck could she do this to us?" said Cash.

"I thought she could have been the one," said Blaze as he looked down at the note and read it over and over.

"Wait a fucking minute, guys. Maybe there's something we're missing," said Zack.

"She fucked us," said Cash, "like she does everyone."

"I thought she was different than what the media said she was, but today, she proved us wrong," said Blaze.

"We can't give up on her," said Zack. "Let's call her to figure out what's going on."

He took out his phone and called Denise. Her phone went straight to voicemail.

"I don't understand," said Zack as he paced back and forth. "There has to be a logical explanation of why she left."

His phone rang. Zack answered it.

"Hello, is this Zack?"

"Yes, who is this?"

"This is Jasmine. I am Denise's sister."

"Hi, Jasmine."

"Have you heard from Denise? It's been a few days since I talked to her, and when I called her today, her phone went to voicemail."

Zack was silent.

"Are you still there?"

"Yes, it's just that she left today and there was a note."

"What? Why would she leave? She said she was happy with you all."

"I don't know. Something is not right.

Jasmine, let me call you back when we have more information."

"Cash, are the cameras still working outside the house? We can see how she left and if she was under any distress."

"Let me check," said Cash.

He pulled out his phone and checked the recorded footage.

"Here it is. Take a look. She got into a black car with tinted windows."

"What the fuck!" yelled Cash.

"Can you see the license plate number in the video?" asked Zack.

"Yes," said Cash. "It's 579234Z."

"Let me call one of my contacts at the station," Blaze said.

He pulled out his phone and called. He gave them the tag numbers.

"Are you able to identify the owner of the car?"

146

"Yes, he has a couple of restraining orders and charges related to kidnapping."

"What the hell! Our girl may have been taken. Can you track the car by traffic light cameras and tolls?"

"It looks like they exited US Highway 1 about an hour ago."

"We are going to check it out. Can you send a patrol just in case?"

"Yes," said the police officer.

Blaze hung up the phone. He relayed the information to Zack and Blaze.

"Let's go," said Zack. "We have a possible location and ID of the car. We can put the two together and see what we come up with. It's worth a try to find Denise."

Blaze tucked his gun into the belt of his pants as they all got into the SUV to search for Denise.

They made it to the location where the black car was last spotted on camera. They drove up and down each street. Then they came to a wooded area and saw a small shack with the black car parked on the side.

"There it is," said Zack.

Zack drove past it and circled around to park about a block away. The element of surprise would be on their side.

Zack led the charge and was in front with Blaze behind and Cash following in the rear. Zack directed Blaze to the left, and he and Cash went to the right of the house. They would meet in the back. Zack looked into the dusty window and saw Denise lying on the floor tied up.

"I see Denise tied up, lying on the floor. She doesn't look hurt, but the windows are so damn dirty I don't have a clear view."

"What is the plan?" said Cash.

"I don't see the stalker. Maybe Blaze has eyes on whoever it is. Let's meet at the rendezvous point at the back of the house."

They ducked under the window and crept to the back of the house where they met Blaze.

"We saw her. She was tied up," said Zack.

"I saw the stalker," said Blaze. "He was taking a fucking shower."

"What's the plan?" asked Cash.

"Let's kick in the door and beat some ass," said Zack. "Cash and I will take the front, and Blaze, you go in through the back door."

"Bet," said Blaze.

"Cash, you grab Denise, and I will go after the stalker with Blaze."

Zack and Cash walked around to the front door, leaving Blaze to the back. One, two, three, and then they kicked in the door. Cash located Denise. Her hands and feet were tied, and she had duct tape around her mouth. Cash removed it first.

"Denise, we are here to help. Are you okay? Did he hurt you?" He inspected the large lump on her head.

"I'm okay. My head hurts, but I'm alive."

He untied her hands and feet.

"The stalker is here, and he said he would hurt me and you guys."

"Don't worry. We can handle this."

By the time, Denise was free, Zack and Blaze had dragged the stalker out of the shower and beat his ass until he was black and blue. He was naked and bruised from head to toe.

"Tie his ass up. The police are here."

Sirens and lights flashed as the police and ambulance parked in front of the house.

"Sergeant, this is Denise. She was kidnapped by the assailant over there. She will need medical attention for the assault," said Zack. "When she's released from the hospital, she can file a statement."

"Sounds like a plan. And where do you three guys come in the picture?"

"We're in a relationship with Denise."

The sergeant tilted his head. His face was marred with confusion. The sergeant left to talk to his captain.

Taking a deep breath, Zack headed toward Denise and his brothers.

"Denise, are you okay? Did he hurt you?"

"I'm okay besides the bump on my head."

"Do you know the guy?"

"Not really. I may have seen him a couple of times on the production set."

"The police are taking him to jail for kidnapping and assault, plus stalking. Are you sure you're okay?"

She went silent for a moment.

"I thought I was going to die. My whole life flashed before my eyes."

Cash moved to her side and wrapped his arms around her shoulders.

"*Renia,* I am so sorry this happened to you. We should have been there for you."

"You were and still are here for me."

Zack and Blaze held her after Cash finished his hug.

The paramedics broke in.

"Hey, guys, we have to take her in for a medical examination. Who's riding in the ambulance with her?"

"I will go with her," said Cash as he helped Denise inside.

"We'll meet you at the hospital," said Zack.

At the hospital, Denise was checked into a patient room. They were keeping her overnight because they wanted to ensure that she didn't have a concussion. The men sat around her bed.

"Don't look at me like I am about to die," said Denise.

"But you could have died or been hurt badly," said Zack. "That stalker guy was a psychopath. We found out that he worked on the set of a number of movies you had been in, and he had set up a shrine for you at his home."

Denise gasped at the newfound knowledge.

"He felt like you had rejected him, but the sick part was he never asked you out. It was all in his head. He threw the dead bird in the window, he hand-delivered the paint-soaked teddy and constantly called you to get your attention."

"That is sick," said Denise.

"But what about the note?" asked Cash. "You said, 'This isn't working.'"

Denise looked down at her hands.

"He told me that he would kill all of you. I left so you wouldn't get hurt."

Cash's face dropped as he looked at Denise. She was willing to sacrifice herself to keep her men safe. The room was silent minus the beep of the machines.

"But three good things did come out of this whole situation. I got to meet three amazing men. Not only did I meet you, but because of your kindness, openness, and the ability to see who I truly was as a person, I am forever changed. No more acting out or like a diva. I figured out it is okay to be my true self and to let people in. Most importantly, I have learned to love. I love you, Zack, Blaze, and Cash."

Happiness and joy surged through her.

"We love you too, Denise. From the first moment our eyes met, I felt a pull to you. I tried to fight it, but it was always there," said Zack.

"I felt the connection when we first touched. I thought it was just a physical attraction, but now I understand it's more. It's love," said Blaze.

"*Renia*, you have always been ours from the start. I know that we would do whatever it takes to keep you as *una familia*. We love you so much."

The guys took turns kissing and hugging their queen and knew in their hearts that she was theirs to love.

Epilogue

One year later.......

Denise walked across the stage to receive her Academy Award for best female actress for the movie *Bad Boys 5*.

"I would like to thank my team for making my dreams a reality. I wouldn't be up here if it wasn't for the support of my family, Jasmine, Zack, Blaze, and Cash."

The audience cheered and clapped. Her men stood behind the curtains ready to act if anything happened to Denise, but today, they were there for moral support only.

A lot had changed since the incident. Denise finished the movie and had a number of gigs set up. She was going all the way to the top, and she had the support to do it.

The men opened two more security firms, and Denise was the face of both. They hired veterans and gave them the opportunity to start a second career. But most importantly, they got to travel with Denise around the world and showed her love at every stop along the way.

Denise walked off stage and straight into their arms.

"Babe, you were amazing out there."

"Thank you, Zack. I have the love and support from my men, and now I can really live out my dreams of being a superstar."

"Denise, you are helping us fulfill our dreams of having a family unit and someone to love us all."

Zack, Cash, and Blaze kissed Denise to show her that they truly loved her and the life they had built.

Read the first book in the series:

"Ours to Hold" The Brotherhood Series: Book 1

Link to book: https://www.amazon.com/dp/B09HVGB6LC

The Lady:

Kiera is a young black data scientist. Her life is threatened when she discovers proof that could destroy her past employer's million-dollar company. While on the run with her new bosses (Troy, Jamal, and Eric) she realizes they are more than just her protectors.

As Kiera runs from one dangerous situation to another, will she lose her heart to all three men along the way?

The Men:
Troy, Jamal, and Eric have been homeboys since back in the day. They have shared women in the past but are looking for more. Will Kiera be what each guy needs or just a one-time thrill ride?

About the Author:
Nia Jolove is an African American author who enjoys writing romance novels, exploring different countries, and singing. She has a passion for the culture and enjoys sharing unconventional stories that reflect it.

Read the second book in the series:

"Ours to Have" The Brotherhood Series: Book 2

Link to book: https://www.amazon.com/dp/B09HVGB6LC

Jasmine, a celebrity hairstylist, and Todd a music producer are about to be married. But before they tie the knot, they agree to a free pass week where they can be single to live out their fantasies without repercussions.

Jasmine's fantasy is to have multiple partners at once. So, she seeks out college friends Jackson, Mike, and Andre.

Jackson, Mike, and Andre have shared women before but are now looking for one woman who would love them all. Years ago, they thought Jasmine may have been the one but she left before they had a chance to explore the connection.

Will what Jasmine shares with three men destroy what she has with Todd? Or will Todd's dark secrets end the marriage before it starts?

Made in United States
North Haven, CT
31 May 2025